Dedication

This book is dedicated to Clementine,
a tiny but mighty chihuahua
who spent her life fighting for shelter animals
and celebrating their humans.

Foreword

This book is intended to be interactive,
to inspire conversations as it is being read.
The illustrations are playful and
sometimes silly, but always intentional.
I hope you enjoy talking about
the Things Lady Likes!

Hello! My name is Lady.
I live with my Mom and we have lots of fun together.
Before that, I was in an animal shelter
with a bunch of other dogs.
We were there for a variety of reasons,
all hoping that someone like my Mom would come and
take us home with them. So you can say I am adopted.
You may know someone who is adopted,
or even be adopted yourself.

I am Lady's Mom. Lady is 13 years old and has been with our family for 10 years.
She is a good girl. She is a good listener, and she even knows a few tricks. There are a lot of things that Lady likes, and she wants to show you some of them.

Lady likes to eat.
She eats all kind of things, even vegetables.
Her favorite vegetable is carrots.

What about you,
do you like vegetables?
What is your favorite vegetable
to eat?

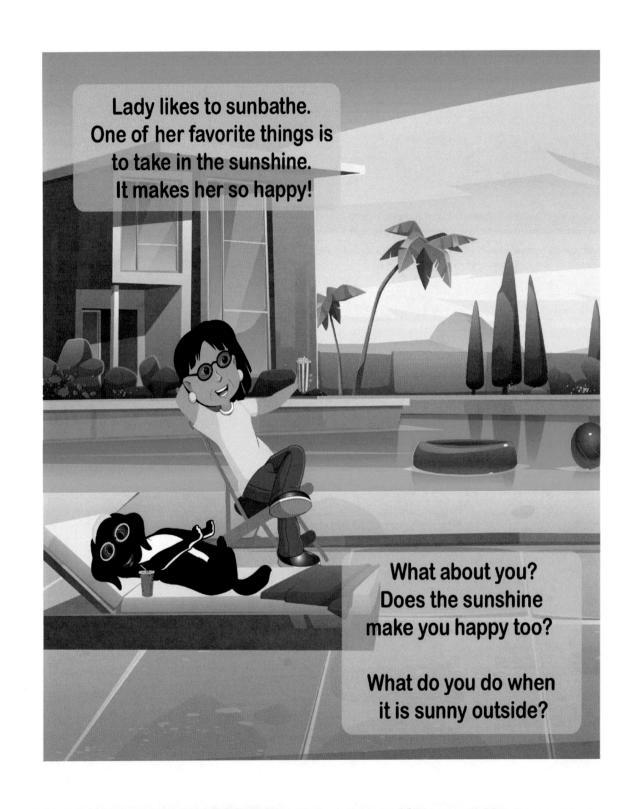

Lady likes to get a bath.
She feels so good when
she is clean and smells nice.

What is your favorite part of bath time?
Do you like taking baths too?

As you can see,
Lady likes many things,
but what she really likes,
is knowing that you both
like many of the same things!

Do you want to share anything
other things that you like?

Things Lady Likes — Activity Pages

Use the Notebook Page to write out
a list of more things that you Like
And then color some of the scenes
from Things Lady Likes

Be sure to share your lists and colorings with us:

IG: @thingsladylikesbook
FB: @thingsladylikesbook
thingsladylikesbook@gmail.com

My List Of Things That I Like

1
2
3
4
5
6
7
8
9
10

About The Author

Donna has lived in Nashville for over 20 years. She is a business leader and active volunteer in the community.

This is her first book in which will hopefully become a series!

Here are some things that Donna likes:

- Fundraising for Nashville Humane Association

- Watching Nashville Predators Hockey

- Listening to Live Music

- Sharing her doggie Lady with all of you